MAX & RUBY'S
TREASURE HUNT

ROSEMARY WELLS

VIKING
An Imprint of Penguin Group (USA) Inc.

For Phoebe and Frances

VIKING
Published by the Penguin Group
Penguin Young Readers Group, 345 Hudson Street, New York, New York 10014, U.S.A.
Penguin Group (Canada), 90 Eglinton Avenue East, Suite 700, Toronto, Ontario, Canada M4P 2Y3
(a division of Pearson Penguin Canada Inc.)
Penguin Books Ltd, 80 Strand, London WC2R 0RL, England
Penguin Ireland, 25 St Stephen's Green, Dublin 2, Ireland (a division of Penguin Books Ltd)
Penguin Group (Australia), 250 Camberwell Road, Camberwell, Victoria 3124, Australia
(a division of Pearson Australia Group Pty Ltd)
Penguin Books India Pvt Ltd, 11 Community Centre, Panchsheel Park, New Delhi – 110 017, India
Penguin Group (NZ), 67 Apollo Drive, Rosedale, Auckland 0632, New Zealand
(a division of Pearson New Zealand Ltd.)
Penguin Books (South Africa) (Pty) Ltd, 24 Sturdee Avenue, Rosebank, Johannesburg 2196, South Africa

Penguin Books Ltd, Registered Offices: 80 Strand, London WC2R 0RL, England

First published in the United States of America by Viking, a division of Penguin Young Readers Group, 2012

1 3 5 7 9 10 8 6 4 2

LIBRARY OF CONGRESS CATALOGING-IN-PUBLICATION DATA
Wells, Rosemary.
Max & Ruby's treasure hunt / by Rosemary Wells.
p. cm.
Summary: When their tea party is rained out, Max and Ruby and their friends
Louise and Lily go indoors, where Grandma has arranged a treasure hunt.
ISBN 978-0-670-06317-8 (hardcover)
[1. Treasure hunt (Game)—Fiction. 2. Rabbits—Fiction. 3. Grandmothers—Fiction.
4. Brothers and sisters—Fiction.] I. Title. II. Title: Max and Ruby's treasure hunt.
PZ7.W46843Marsm 2012
[E]—dc23
2011048535

Manufactured in China   Set in Minister
The art for this book was rendered in ink, watercolor, and gouache.

ALWAYS LEARNING   PEARSON

"Let's have a tea party!" said Max's sister, Ruby.
"Good idea!" said Ruby's best friend, Louise.
There was not a cloud in the sky. But suddenly . . .

went the thunderstorm, just when Ruby was pouring a cup
of pretend tea for Louise's little sister, Lily.

Lily grabbed her doll, Dagmar, and everybody ran into the house as fast as they could.

"Rain rain, go away!" said Ruby.
"Come again another day!" said Louise.

"Everybody wants to play!" chimed in Max.
Grandma heard every word.

"Let's have a treasure hunt!" said Grandma.
"How does it work?" asked Louise.
"There are seven clues hidden in seven places in the house," said Grandma. "Follow the clues, one after another, and you will find the treasure!"

"Where do we begin?" asked Ruby.
"Let me see!" said Grandma.
"Let's start with 'Cock-a-doodle-doo.
My dame has lost her . . .' oh dear! something or other!
Who can think of what she lost?"

"What rhymes with cock-a-doodle-doo?" asked Ruby.
"My dame has lost her SHOE!" said Louise.
"Look!" shouted Lily.

"There's a Max sneaker under the chair!"
Sure enough, under the easy chair was Max's
blue sneaker. Inside was the first clue.

Ruby read it out loud.

I'm a little _____,
short and stout.
Tip me over and
pour me out!

"I know! I know! I know!" said Louise.
She looked in the dining room cupboard. She took
out the teapot. Inside the teapot was the second clue!
Louise read it.

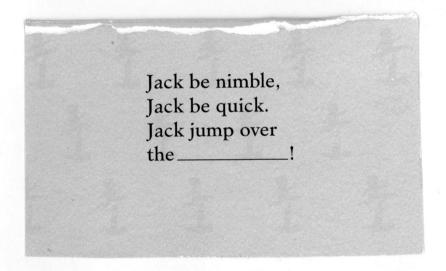

Jack be nimble,
Jack be quick.
Jack jump over
the _____!

Everyone guessed what might rhyme with quick.
Lily got it right.

The third clue was in the hall under one of the candlesticks.

Lily found it. She could not read yet so Louise read it for her.

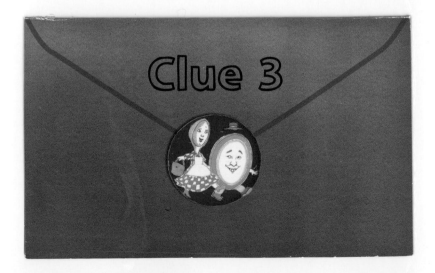

"It has to rhyme with moon," said Ruby.
This time Max guessed right.

Max was the first one to get to the pantry silverware drawer. Sure enough, in the spoon slot was the next clue.

"Hooray!" shouted Max.
Max couldn't read the clue, so Ruby had to do it for him.

"This one isn't a rhyming clue," said Ruby.
"What could Miss Mary Mack have down her back?" asked Louise.

Everyone had an idea. But Lily knew the rhyme by heart.

She led the way upstairs to the closet.

On the shelf was Grandma's sewing box.
"Silver buttons!" said Louise.
In the sewing box was another clue.

Little Boy Blue
come blow your _____!
The sheep's in the meadow,
the cow's in the corn.

"What could it be?" asked Louise.
"Blow your horn? How about the car horn?" asked Ruby.
"Garage!" said Max.

Ruby was right!

On the steering wheel of Grandma's red Chevrolet was the next clue.

Ruby pushed the button and put the top down.
The clue said:

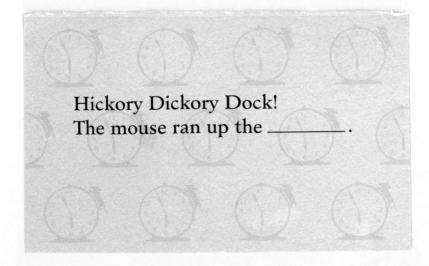

Hickory Dickory Dock!
The mouse ran up the _____.

"Dock," said Louise. "What rhymes with dock?"

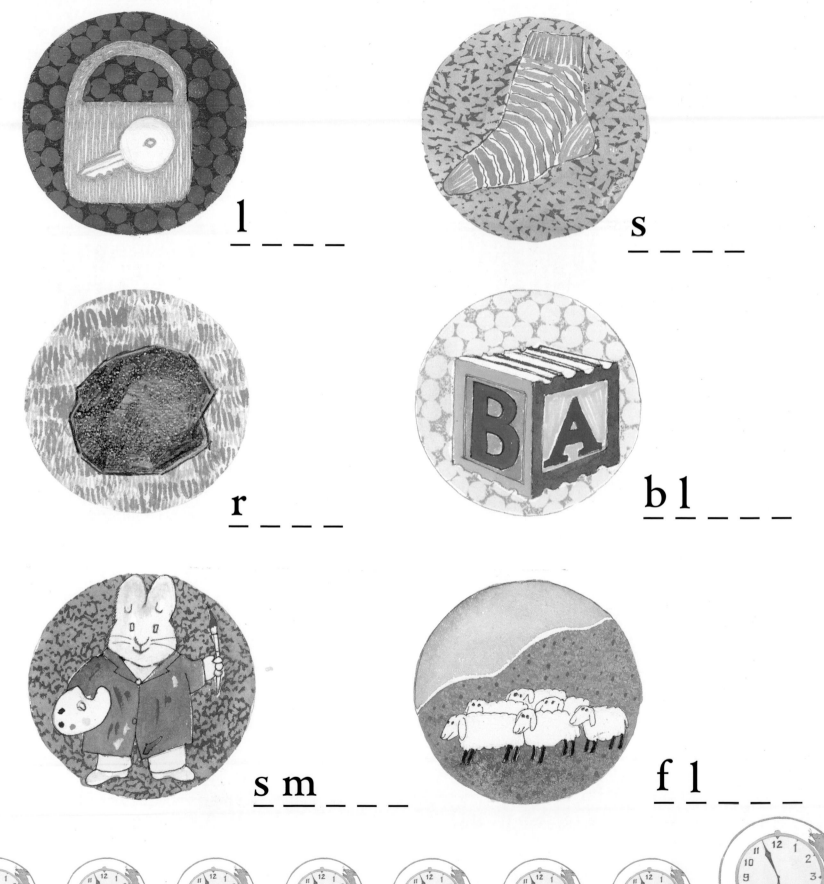

l _ _ _ _

s _ _ _ _

r _ _ _

b l _ _ _ _

s m _ _ _ _

f l _ _ _ _

"Clock!" said Max.

But there was nothing under the alarm clock in the bedroom.

There was nothing under the clock radio in the guest room.

Suddenly Louise heard it . . .

It was the grandfather clock in the living room.

Downstairs they all went.
Ruby opened the door of the big grandfather clock.
Inside was the last clue. It said:

Pussycat, pussycat,
where have you been?
I've been to London
to visit the queen.
Pussycat, pussycat,
what did you there?
I frightened a little mouse
under ___ _____.

Max bolted for the screened porch.
He opened the door.

Under Grandma's chair was the treasure box!
Max was the first to open it.
Inside were five gold coins filled with chocolate.
"They are too beautiful to eat," said Ruby.

"But there are only four of us and five coins!" said Louise.

"One for Dagmar!" said Grandma.
"Dagmar!" Lily shouted. "Where is Dagmar?"
"Did you leave her in one of the clue locations?"
said Grandma.

"Maybe, but which one?" said Ruby.

Dining room, hall, pantry, closet, garage, bedroom, living room!

There were so many clues and different locations.

No one could remember where Dagmar might have been lost.

Is Dagmar in the dining room?

Is Dagmar in the hall?

Is Dagmar in the pantry?

Is Dagmar in the closet?

Is Dagmar in the garage?

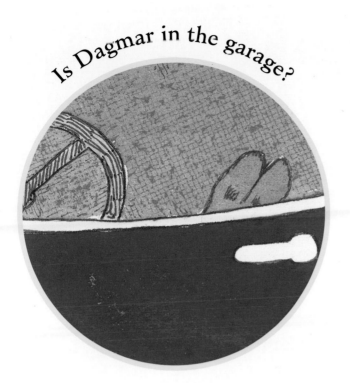

Is Dagmar in the bedroom?

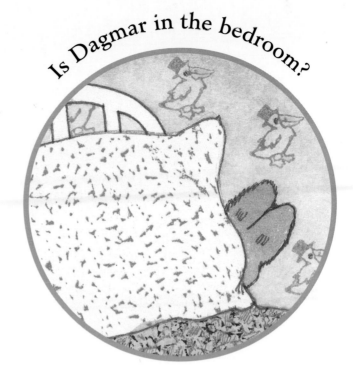

Is Dagmar in the living room?

No! Max found Dagmar . . .

in the parlor, right where Lily left her! Hurray!